ELIVIA SAVADIER

NO HAIRCUT TODAY!

A NEAL PORTER BOOK
ROARING BROOK PRESS
BROOKFIELD, CONNECTICUT

For Marie, Jean Pierre of Salon Joli,
and for Dominic.

Distributed in Canada by H. B. Fenn and Company Ltd.

Library of Congress Cataloging-in-Publication Data:
Savadier, Elivia.
No haircut today / written and illustrated by Elivia Savadier.
p. cm.
"A Neal Porter book."
Summary: Dominic refuses to get his hair cut, no matter how much his mother wants him to or how bad it looks.
ISBN 1-59643-046-X
[1. Haircutting—Fiction.   2. Mothers and sons—Fiction.]   I. Title.
PZ7.S2584No 2005
[E]—dc22   2004017638

Roaring Brook Press books are available for special promotions and premiums.
For details contact: Director of Special Markets, Holtzbrinck Publishers.

Printed in China
2   4   6   8   10   9   7   5   3   1

This is Dominic's hair.

Dominic's hair is

LONG

in some spots and

SHORT

in other spots.

Some parts are

curly.

Other parts are

STRAIGHT.

He does **not** like to have his

HAIR CUT.

Will he have it cut in a **car** chair?

NO!

How about an **airplane** chair?

NO!

His mom **loves** to cut people's hair.

She cuts their hair and curls their hair. They look great.

When Dominic sees

SCISSORS

he screams!

If **anyone** tries to hold his head

no matter how gently

he screams!

His mother gets
VERY UPSET.

"MOMMY!

Are you mad at me?" he asks.

"I'm not mad at you," she whispers. "I love you."

"I love you, too," he says.

Her hair is cut just right. His hair isn't cut at all.
Their faces touch. Their hair gets all

MIXED UP!

NO HAIRCUT TODAY!

Their eyes sparkle and they laugh.

Maybe . . .

tomorrow.